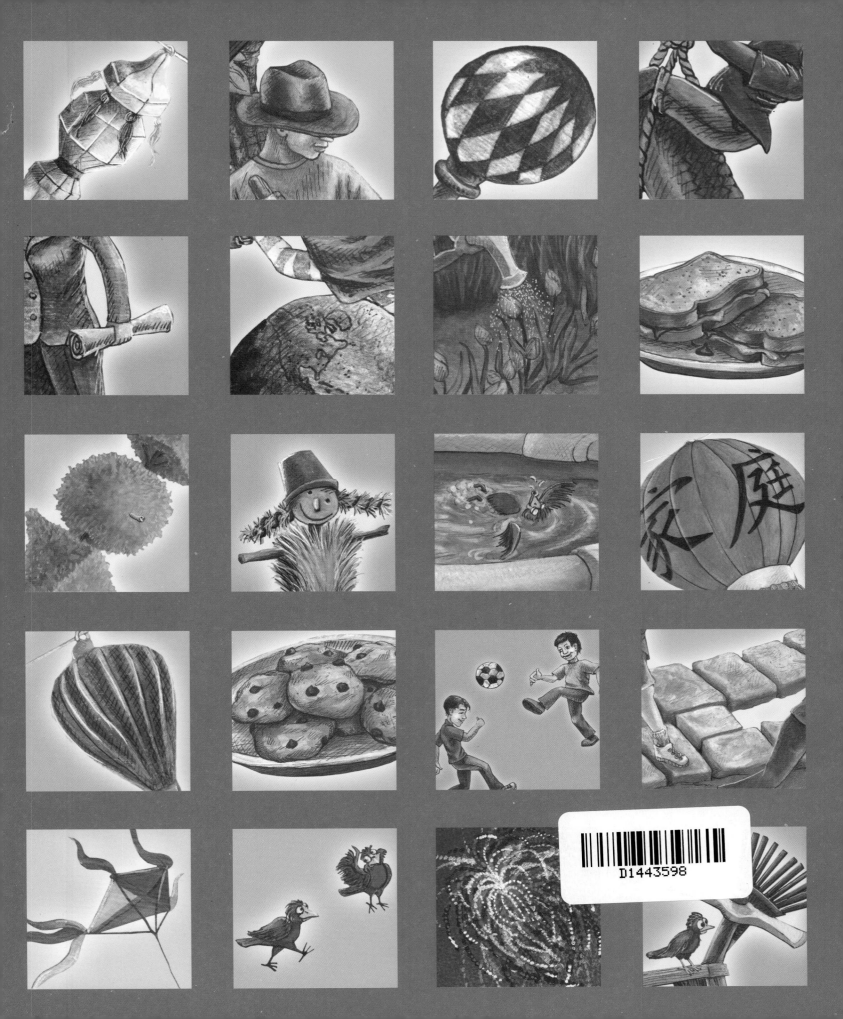

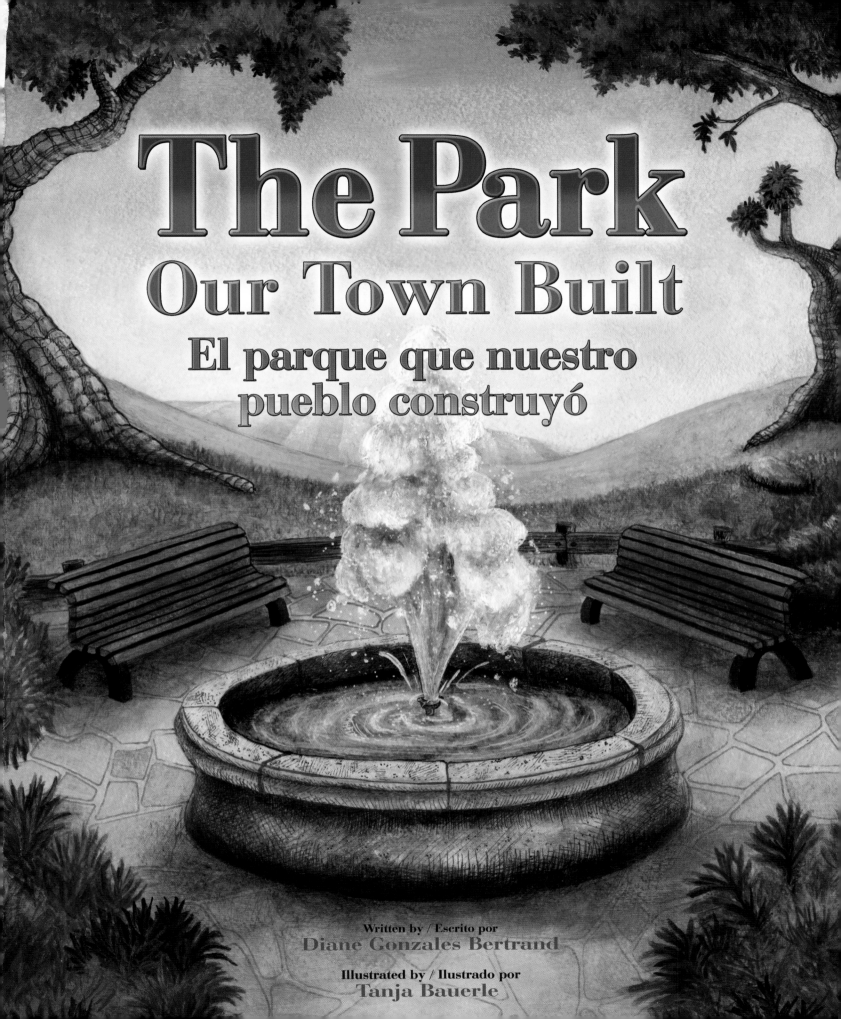

The Park
Our Town Built
El parque que nuestro pueblo construyó

Written by / Escrito por
Diane Gonzales Bertrand

Illustrated by / Ilustrado por
Tanja Bauerle

For Renée, Barry, Matthew, and Kyle, with love.
- Diane

**For my shining stars –
Kevin, Isabelle, and Zoe.**
- Tanja

Bertrand, Diane Gonzales.

The Park Our Town Built / written by Diane Gonzales Bertrand: illustrated by Tanja Bauerle; translated by Cambridge BrickHouse = El parque que nuestro pueblo construyó / escrito por Diane Gonzales Bertrand; ilustrado por Tanja Bauerle; traducción al español de Cambridge BrickHouse —1 ed. — McHenry, IL ; Raven Tree Press, 2011.

p. cm.

SUMMARY: In this cumulative story, townspeople work together to build a park and then celebrate their achievement with fireworks and a party.

Bilingual Edition
ISBN 978-1-936299-12-6 hardcover
English Edition
ISBN 978-1-936299-14-0 hardcover

Audience: pre–K to 3rd grade.
Title available in bilingual English-Spanish (concept words only) or English-only editions.

1. Parks--Fiction. 2. City and town life--Fiction. 3. Spanish language materials--Bilingual.] I. Bauerle, Tanja, 1970- ill. II. Title. III. Title: Parque que nuestro pueblo construyó.

Library of Congress Control Number: 2010936677

Printed in the USA
10 9 8 7 6 5 4 3 2
First Edition

**Free activities for this book are available at
www.raventreepress.com**

Raven Tree Press
A Division of Delta Systems Co., Inc.
www.raventreepress.com

This is the park our town built.

This is the man

who gave us the land

for *el parque* our town built.

5

This is the mayor

who spoke to *el hombre*
who gave us *la tierra*
for *el parque* our town built.

These are the children

who went with *la alcaldesa*
who spoke to *el hombre*
who gave us *la tierra*
for *el parque* our town built.

These are the people

who helped *los niños*
who went with *la alcaldesa*
who spoke to *el hombre*
who gave us *la tierra*
for *el parque* our town built.

These are the tools

carried by *la gente*
who helped *los niños*
who went with *la alcaldesa*
who spoke to *el hombre*
who gave us *la tierra*
for *el parque* our town built.

These are the swings

made with *las herramientas*
carried by *la gente*
who helped *los niños*
who went with *la alcaldesa*
who spoke to *el hombre*
who gave us *la tierra*
for *el parque* our town built.

This is the slide

to match *los columpios*
made with *las herramientas*
carried by *la gente*
who helped *los niños*
who went with *la alcaldesa*
who spoke to *el hombre*
who gave us *la tierra*
for *el parque* our town built.

17

This is the bridge

built near *el tobogán*
to match *los columpios*
made with *las herramientas*
carried by *la gente*
who helped *los niños*
who went with *la alcaldesa*
who spoke to *el hombre*
who gave us *la tierra*
for *el parque* our town built.

19

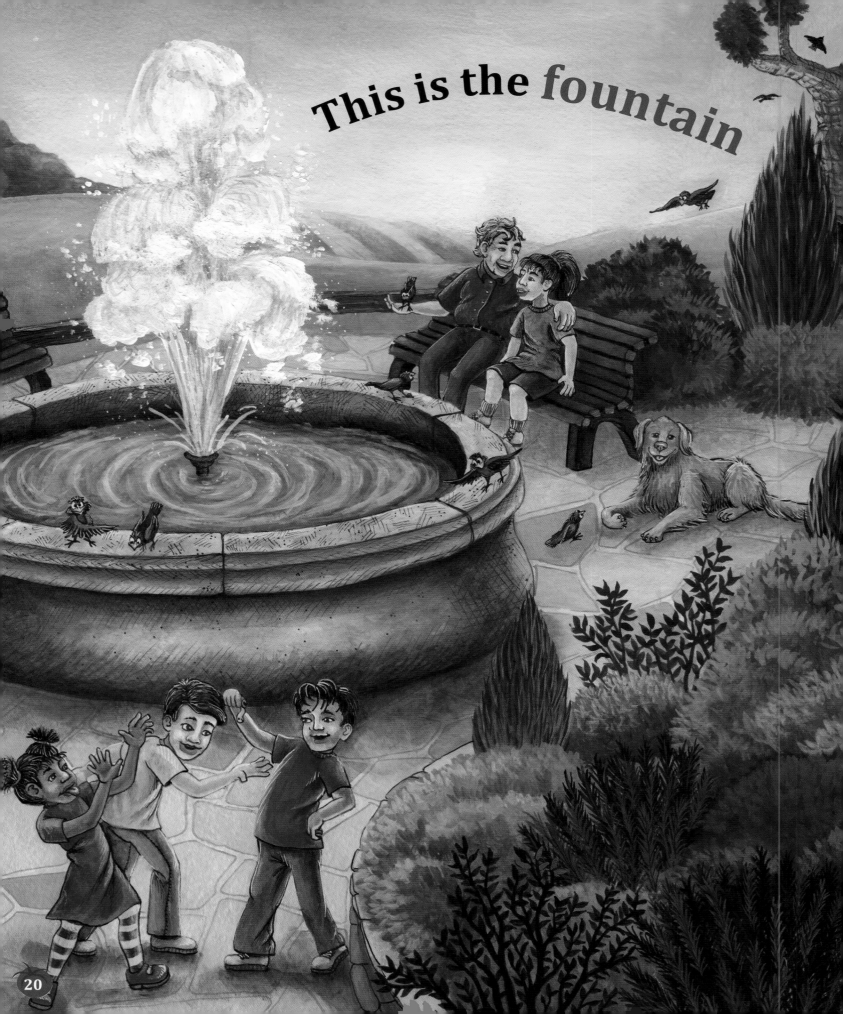

This is the fountain

behind *el puente*
built near *el tobogán*
to match *los columpios*
made with *las herramientas*
carried by *la gente*
who helped *los niños*
who went with *la alcaldesa*
who spoke to *el hombre*
who gave us *la tierra*
for *el parque* our town built.

These are the benches

that circle *la fuente*
behind *el puente*
built near *el tobogán*
to match *los columpios*
made with *las herramientas*
carried by *la gente*
who helped *los niños*
who went with *la alcaldesa*
who spoke to *el hombre*
who gave us *la tierra*
for *el parque* our town built.

This is the garden

that grows near *los bancos*
that circle *la fuente*
behind *el puente*
built near *el tobogán*
to match *los columpios*
made with *las herramientas*
carried by *la gente*
who helped *los niños*
who went with *la alcaldesa*
who spoke to *el hombre*
who gave us *la tierra*
for *el parque* our town built.

These are the families

who planted *el jardín*
that grows near *los bancos*
that circle *la fuente*
behind *el puente*
built near *el tobogán*
to match *los columpios*
made with *las herramientas*
carried by *la gente*
who helped *los niños*
who went with *la alcaldesa*
who spoke to *el hombre*
who gave us *la tierra*
for *el parque* our town built.

This is the party

for all of *las familias*
who planted *el jardín*
that grows near *los bancos*
that circle *la fuente*
behind *el puente*
built near *el tobogán*
to match *los columpios*
made with *las herramientas*
carried by *la gente*
who helped *los niños*
who went with *la alcaldesa*
who spoke to *el hombre*
who gave us *la tierra*
for *el parque* our town built.

These are the fireworks

that go off at *la fiesta*
for all of *las familias*
who planted *el jardín*
that grows near *los bancos*
that circle *la fuente*
behind *el puente*
built near *el tobogán*
to match *los columpios*
made with *las herramientas*
carried by *la gente*
who helped *los niños*
who went with *la alcaldesa*
who spoke to *el hombre*
who gave us *la tierra*
for *el parque*   our town built.

Vocabulary Page

English	Spanish
the park	*el parque*
the land	*la tierra*
the man	*el hombre*
the mayor	*la alcaldesa*
the children	*los niños*
the people	*la gente*
the tools	*las herramientas*
the swings	*los columpios*
the slide	*el tobogán*
the bridge	*el puente*
the fountain	*la fuente*
the benches	*los bancos*
the garden	*el jardín*
the families	*las familias*
the party	*la fiesta*